JACK's TRACTOR

by Thomas Taylor
Illustrated by John Kelly
First published in 2009 by Hodder Children's Books
This edition published in 2010

Text copyright © Thomas Taylor 2009
Illustration copyright © John Kelly 2009
Hodder Children's Books
338 Euston Road, London, NW1 3BH

Hodder Children's Books Australia
Level 17/207 Kent Street, Sydney, NSW 2000

The right of Thomas Taylor to be identified as the author and John Kelly as the
illustrator of this Work has been asserted by them in accordance with the
Copyright, Designs and Patents Act 1988.

A catalogue record of this book is
available from the British Library.

ISBN: 978 0 340 95707 3
10 9 8 7 6 5 4 3 2

Printed in China

Hodder Children's Books is a division of Hachette Children's Books.
An Hachette UK Company.

www.hachette.co.uk

For Aunty Gemily – T.T.

To Paul, who fixed my arms and made this book possible.

To Cathy, for putting up with me while I was out of order. – J.K.

Thomas Taylor

Jack's Tractor

Illustrated by John Kelly

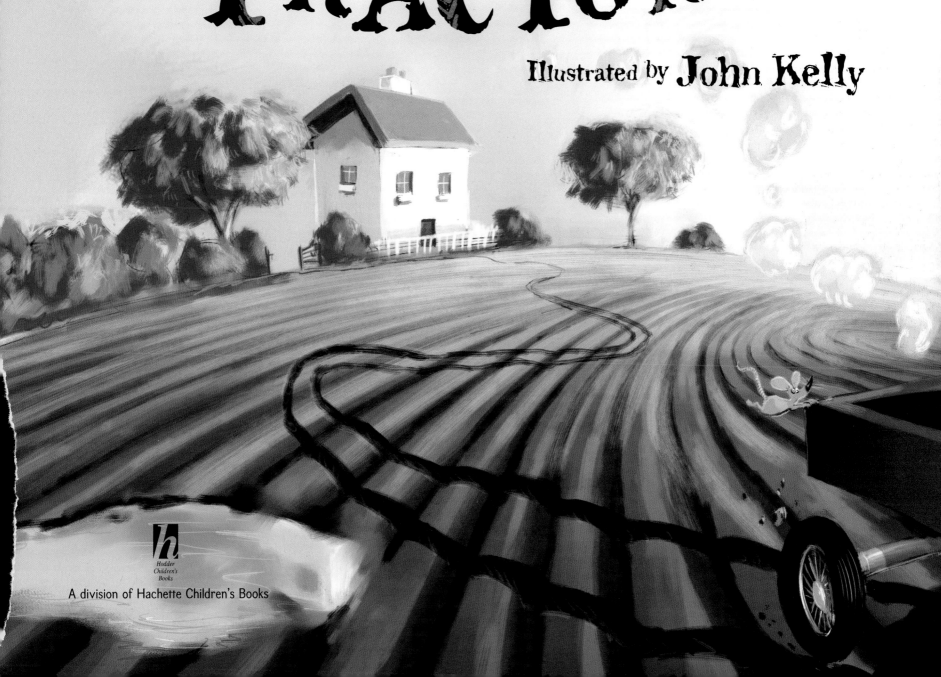

Hodder Children's Books

A division of Hachette Children's Books

Here's Jack! His tractor's big and red,
His trailer's fixed behind.
'I'm going for a ride,' he said,
'To see what I can find.'

BRUM-BRUM!
VRUUUM!

Squeak!

He held the wheel, he shook the ground,
He roared the engine's noise.
It's just the sort of noisy sound
That pleases little boys.

He drove the tractor to a farm
And horrified the hens.
The sheep all bleated in alarm,
The pigs broke from their pens.

BRUM-BRUM!

But then he heard a silly sound –
  A honk all wild and wonky.
Reversing gear, he backed around
  And loaded up a donkey!

HEE-HAWR!

He drove the tractor
through the zoo
And scattered the giraffes.

The grizzly bears were
scared off too,
Though monkeys got
their laughs.

SQUAWK!

But when he heard the parrot's shriek,
Jack knew just what to do.
He caught him by his orange beak
And loaded him up too!

HEE-HAWR!

BRUM-BRUM!

Squeak!

He drove the tractor to a swamp -
A prehistoric glade.

SQUAWK!

HEE-HAWR!

BRUM-BRUM!

Squeak!

He made the giant monsters stomp
With all the noise he made.

TICKLE-PICKLE!

Then suddenly
a beast jumped out,
A wriggly Ticklesaur!

He tickled Jack. Jack tickled him,
Then shut the trailer door.

He drove his tractor to the plains
  Where lions growled and roared.
He had to drive it very fast
  To get a lion on-board.

BARGH-WARGH!

Squeak!

Then in Antarctic icy wastes
He heard a walrus bellow.
He slid the tractor to a stop
To load the splendid fellow.

Squeak!

By now the tractor creaked and groaned
    With all this noisy weight,
So Jack turned round to head off home
    Before it got too late.

But as the sun went quickly down,
And darkness closed the day,
Jack stopped the tractor, looked around –

'I do not know the way!'

Then suddenly out jumped a mouse,

'I know just what to do.
I'll lead you straight back to your house -
All day I've followed you.

But listen, now that night has come,
You mustn't make such noise.
It's bedtime now - we need our sleep.
Yes, even little boys.'

Squeak!

They drove back through
the icy waste,
Where Walrus was
quite quiet.

Bogh!

Then over plains
they ranged again,
But Lion made
no riot.

Grrrr!

And as they crossed the boggy swamp,
The Ticklesaur just waved.

The parrot, and the donkey too,
Were very well behaved.

Till in the end they came back home –
Now what a noisy day!
'And thank you, Mouse, for helping out
And showing us the way.

And though you don't go BRUM or BRAY
Or SQUAWK or GROWL or ROAR,
little squeak has saved the day,'
Jack. And Mouse said...

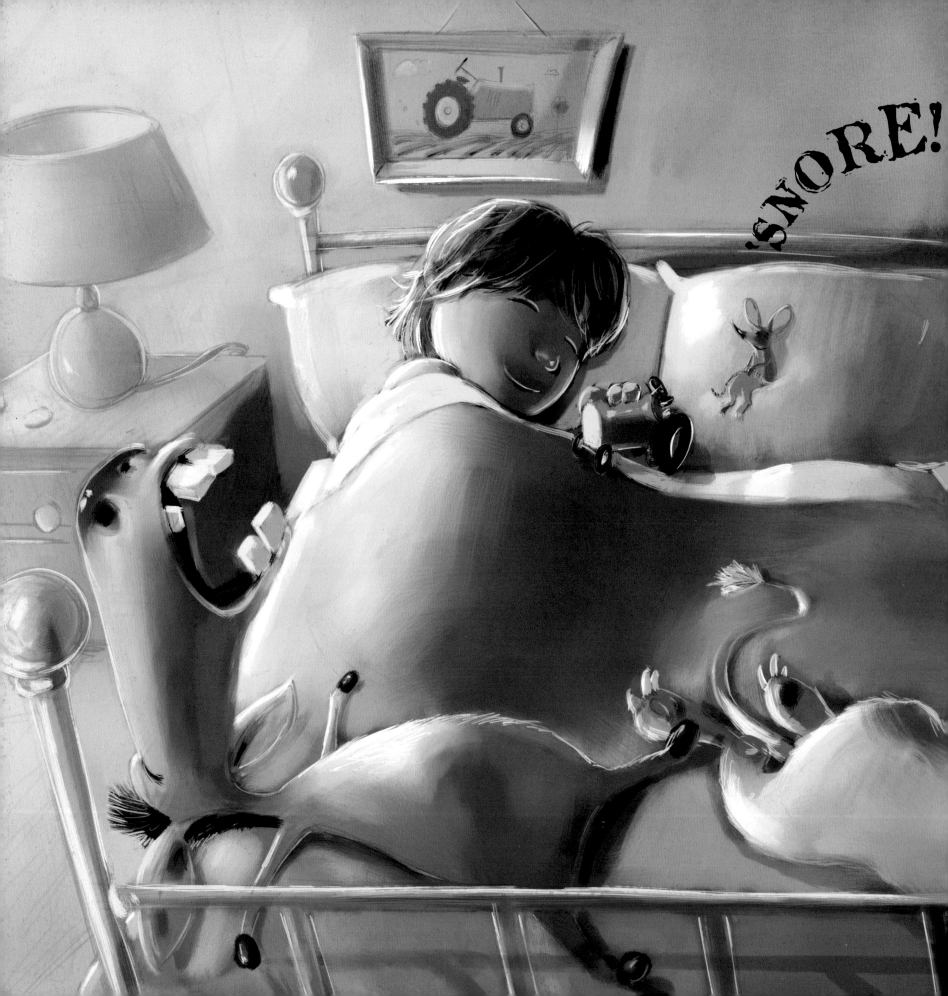

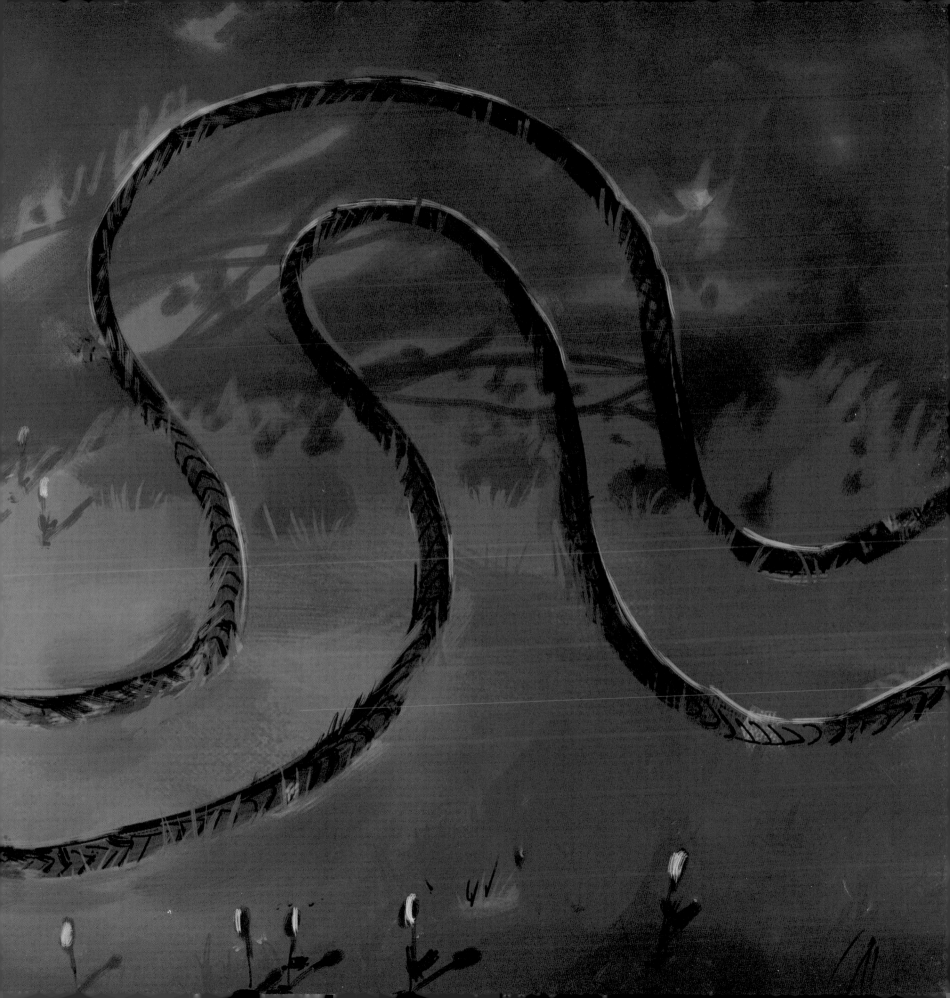

Other great Hodder picture books perfect to share with children:

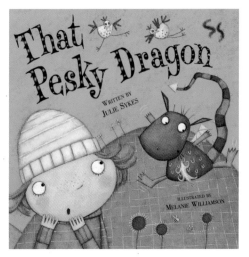

978 0 340 93200 1

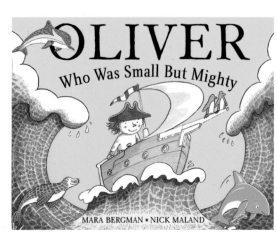

978 0 340 93055 7

978 0 340 93242 1

978 0 340 94508 7

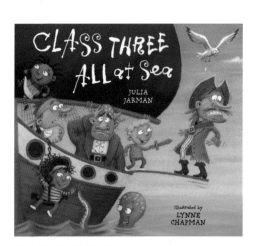

978 0 340 94466 0

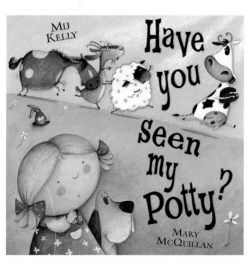

978 0 340 91153 2

Hodder
Children's
Books

A division of Hachette Children's Books